HARPER
An Imprint of HarperCollinsPublishers www.harpercollinschildrens.com   Illustrations © 2019 by James Dean

Pete the Cat

The Great Leprechaun Chase

by James Dean

HARPER

An Imprint of HarperCollinsPublishers

Pete the Cat: The Great Leprechaun Chase
Copyright © 2019 by James Dean
Pete the Cat is a registered trademark of Pete the Cat, LLC.
All rights reserved. Manufactured in China.
No part of this book may be used or reproduced in any manner whatsoever without written
permission except in the case of brief quotations embodied in critical articles and reviews. For
information address HarperCollins Children's Books, a division of HarperCollins Publishers, 195
Broadway, New York, NY 10007.
www.harpercollinschildrens.com

Library of Congress Control Number: 2018945991
ISBN 978-0-06-240450-3

The artist used pen and ink, with watercolor and acrylic paint, on
300lb hot press paper to create the illustrations for this book.
Typography by Honee Jang
18 19 20 21 22 SCP 10 9 8 7 6 5 4 3 2 1

First Edition

Tomorrow is St. Patrick's Day, and Pete's teacher,
Mr. G., is teaching about leprechauns.
  "The only time you can catch one is on St. Patrick's Day.
A leprechaun will bring you good luck!" Mr. G. says.

Now everyone in class wants a leprechaun.
  Pete gets a great idea. He will open a leprechaun
catching business!

St. Patrick's Day comes, and Pete gathers some supplies.

He hangs a sign above his stand.

This will be easy, Pete thinks.

Squirrel is Pete's first customer.
"I want a leprechaun," Squirrel says.
"I need good luck for my test!"

"Cool. I'm on it,"
says Pete.

Pete has a plan. He will follow a
rainbow until he finds a leprechaun.

Finally, Pete arrives at the end of the rainbow and finds Clover the leprechaun next to a pot of gold. Pete sneaks up behind Clover.

SWOOSH!

But Clover is too fast!
"Did you think you could catch me so easily?" he asks.

Once there was a cat named Pete,
Who thought nabbing some luck would be neat.
Then he happened upon
A smart leprechaun,
Who he'll find quite tricky to beat.

Clover disappears in a puff of green smoke. Pete will need a new plan.

That afternoon, Gus visits Pete's Lucky Leprechaun Catchers. "I want a leprechaun," Gus says. "I need good luck for my band recital!"

Pete says, "I'll see what I can do."

To: _____

From: _____

To: _____

From: _____

To: _____

From: _____

To: _____

From: _____

To: _____

From: _____

To: _____

From: _____

To: _____

From: _____

To: _____

From: _____

To: _____

From: _____

To: _____

From: _____

To: _____

From: _____

To: _____

From: _____

Pete plans to lure Clover out with his music.
He plays a jaunty song on his guitar. Before long,
Clover dances over to Pete.
Just a little closer, Pete thinks.

Suddenly, Clover starts spinning around Pete.
Round and round, Clover goes faster and faster!

Oh no! Clover wraps up Pete with the rope!

Pete has finally met his match,
A crafty leprechaun he just can't catch.
He'll never win!
He better give in.
Or find something else to snatch!

That evening, Callie visits Pete's Lucky Leprechaun Catchers.
"I want a leprechaun," Callie says. "I need good luck
for my tennis match."

"Hmm," says Pete.
St. Patrick's Day is almost over. There isn't
much time left to catch a leprechaun.
But Pete won't give up yet.

Pete sets a trap for Clover. Before long, Clover tiptoes up to the trap and sniffs the air.

"Mmm, I love candy," he whispers, peering under the box.

Pete waits very quietly.

CRASH! Pete rushes over and checks underneath the trap. But it is empty!

Clover skips away.

Pete has tried many a plot,
But still I haven't been caught!
And isn't it dandy,
I even got candy,
While Pete ends up with squat!

Pete has an idea. He follows the trail of spilled candy to Clover's secret hideout.

Pete sneaks up behind Clover.

Pete finally catches Clover!

"Why do you want me?" Clover asks.
"I'm helping my friends who need
some extra luck," Pete says.

"Luck doesn't come from having a leprechaun," says Clover.
"You and your friends have each other. That already makes
you as lucky as can be."

Could Clover be right?
Pete is one very lucky cat. A lucky cat doesn't need a lucky leprechaun!

He lets Clover go.

Pete decides he will be the good luck his friends need by helping them out himself.

Pete helps Squirrel study for his test.
Squirrel aces it!

Pete helps Gus rehearse for the recital.
Gus rocks it!

Pete helps Callie practice
for her match.
Callie wins it!

Clover magically appears.
"Good job, Pete!"
says Clover.
"I have one more poem
for you!"

While Clover played hide-and-seek
Pete learned something unique.
The luck that you make
Beats luck that you take
Any ol' day of the week!

Happy St. Patrick's Day!